THE JOKER'S BIG BREAK

Story by Michael Petranek

Based on the screenplay by
Seth Grahame-Smith, Chris McKenna
and Erik Sommers, with additional
material by Jared Stern and
John Whittington.

Based on LEGO® Construction Toys.

■ SCHOLASTIC

Scholastic Children's Books
Euston House,
24 Eversholt Street,
London NW1 1DB, UK

A division of Scholastic Ltd
London ~ New York ~ Toronto ~ Sydney ~ Auckland
Mexico City ~ New Delhi ~ Hong Kong

This book was first published in the US in 2017 by Scholastic Inc.
Published in the UK by Scholastic Ltd, 2017

ISBN 978 1407 17725 0

Based on the Screenplay by Chris McKenna & Erik Sommers with additional material by Jared Stern, John Whittington and Seth Grahame-Smith

2 4 6 8 10 9 7 5 3 1

Printed in China

Papers used by Scholastic Children's Books are made from wood grown in responsible forests.

www.scholastic.co.uk

Ha! Ha! Ha!

I don't need to introduce myself, do I? I'm the Joker, and I'm the greatest bad guy Batman has ever faced. I'm here to tell you how I outsmarted Batman with my genius plan to take over Gotham City!

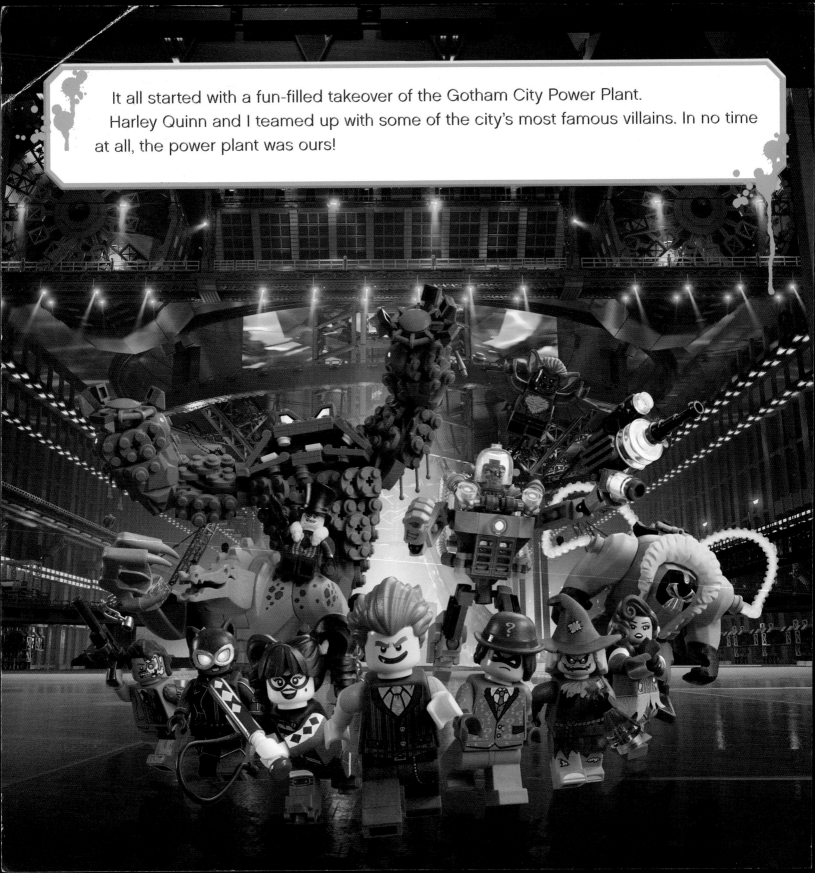

It all started with a fun-filled takeover of the Gotham City Power Plant. Harley Quinn and I teamed up with some of the city's most famous villains. In no time at all, the power plant was ours!

A Joker bomb – that's trademarked – was attached to the energy core by some of the Penguin's, um... brothers? Pets? I don't know how that works. Anyways, there was a bunch of little penguins and they put the bomb there – that's what matters.

With the push of a button from yours truly, the city would become the Joker's Fun Zone. Ha! Ha! Ha!

I told the police that we wanted the mayor – and they gave her to us! She was there to hand over the city.

Gotham City was ours! We had won!

Of course, because nothing is ever easy, Batman showed up to save the day. He pumped some phat beatz from his Let's Get Nuts playlist to get him in the mood. My henchmen and I couldn't believe our eyes. Or ears.

PLAYLISTS

Gym Workout

Super Cool Mega Mix

LET'S GET NUTS Mix

Batman Solos

Well, you can guess what happened next. He jumped around, threw a bunch of Batarangs at my henchmen and, before I knew it, it was just him and me.
I wasn't going to hang around any longer than I needed to!

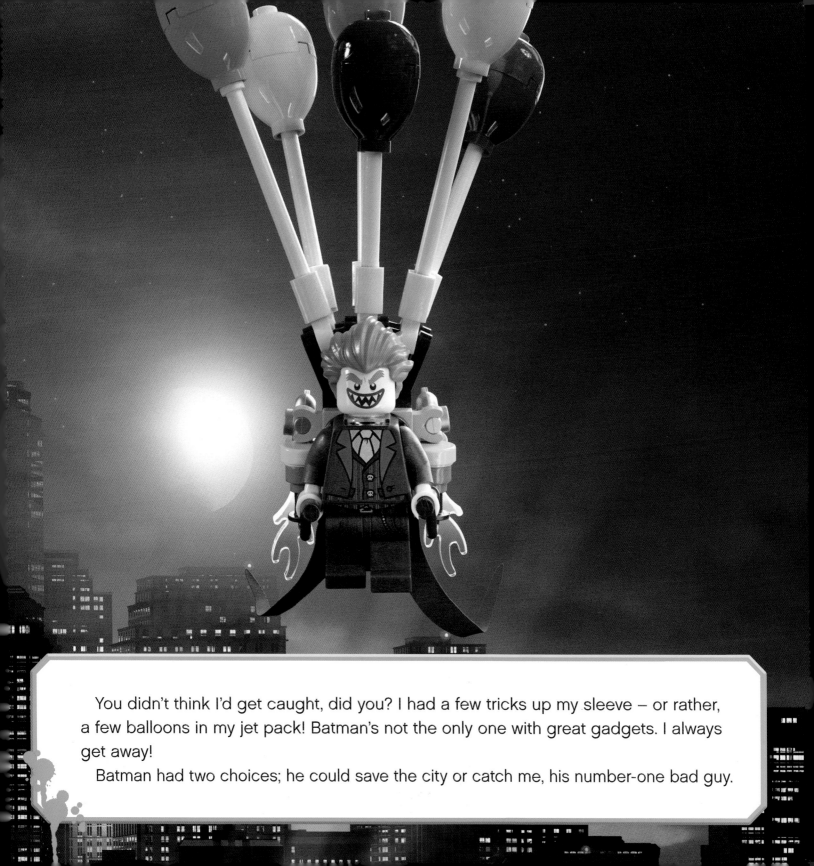

You didn't think I'd get caught, did you? I had a few tricks up my sleeve – or rather, a few balloons in my jet pack! Batman's not the only one with great gadgets. I always get away!

Batman had two choices; he could save the city or catch me, his number-one bad guy.

That's when things got a little not so funny.

"You're not my number-one bad guy," Batman said. "You never have been and you never will be. There's nothing special about us."

Ouch.

Well, that wasn't very nice.

Of course I'm Batman's number-one bad guy! I mean, he spends so much time chasing me, we're practically best friends!

I flew back to my hideout.

I decided to just veg out, watch some TV.

What Batman said to me really hurt.

I might be a super-villain, but I still have feelings!

That's when I saw something very interesting on TV – Superman.

Superman had just sent his greatest enemy, Zod, to a place called the Phantom Zone.

"Now that he's gone," Superman said, "I think I'm going to miss him. I couldn't put Zod in just a normal prison. I had to send him to the most secure prison, home of all the universe's most notorious bad guys... the Phantom Zone."

That's when I got a new plan! It was a bold one.

It's like Harley Quinn says, "Sometimes, Mr J., the best way to get something you really, really want is to act like you don't want it at all!"

All those bad guys in one place have a lot of advice to give!

That night, there was a big party for Commissioner Gordon. He was retiring, and his daughter was taking over!

Everyone would be there – the mayor, the commissioner, Bruce Wayne...

It was the perfect opportunity to get some more one-on-one time with Batman, and put my plan in motion!

Just look at us! We sure know how to make an entrance.

I knew that with Harley Quinn and me on the scene, it wouldn't be long before we got an appearance from Batman.

Harley and I split up for the next part of our plan.

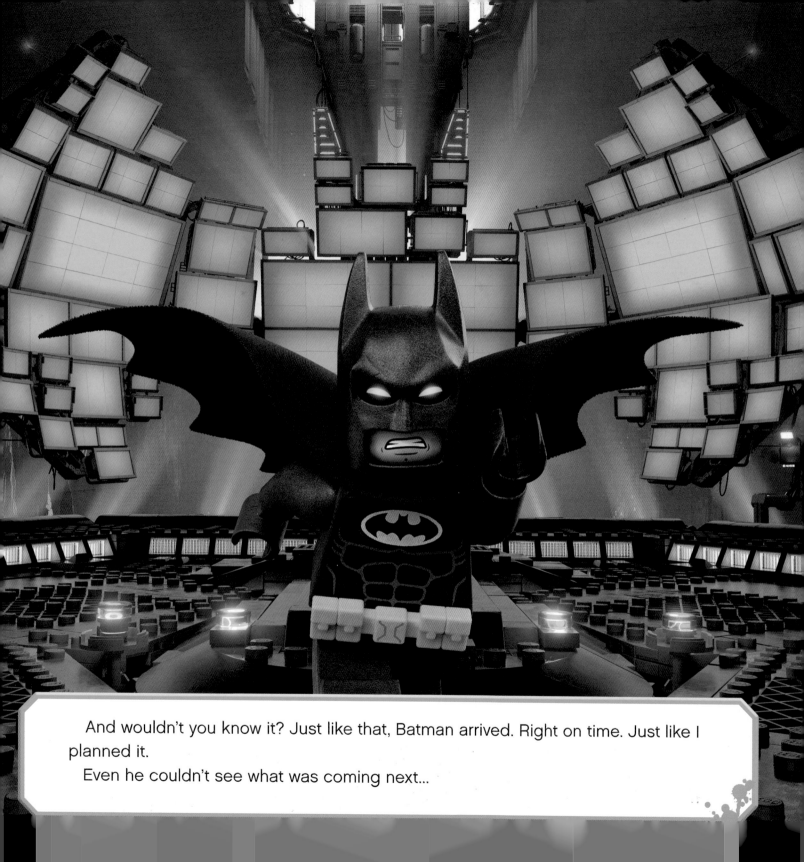

And wouldn't you know it? Just like that, Batman arrived. Right on time. Just like I planned it.

Even he couldn't see what was coming next...

I surrendered!

Batman couldn't believe it.

I told the police to take me to Arkham Asylum. Batman thought I was up to something. Of course, I was.

"The Joker wants to go to Arkham Asylum! That's the last place he should want to go. Unless he's got a plan," said Batman.

Right when they let me out, a loud voice from the crowd planted an idea in Batman's head.

"What if you put him in the PZ?" the voice said.

"The Phantom Zone! That's a great idea," Batman replied.

Little did Batman know the voice was Harley Quinn's, and it was part of my plan. Now all I had to do was wait at Arkham Asylum...

No sooner was I settled into my cell, when I heard sirens outside. Batman was making his way to my cell, and the guards were not happy he was going around them to get me.

"Attention, all inmates! We're on high alert! Return to your cells immediately!"

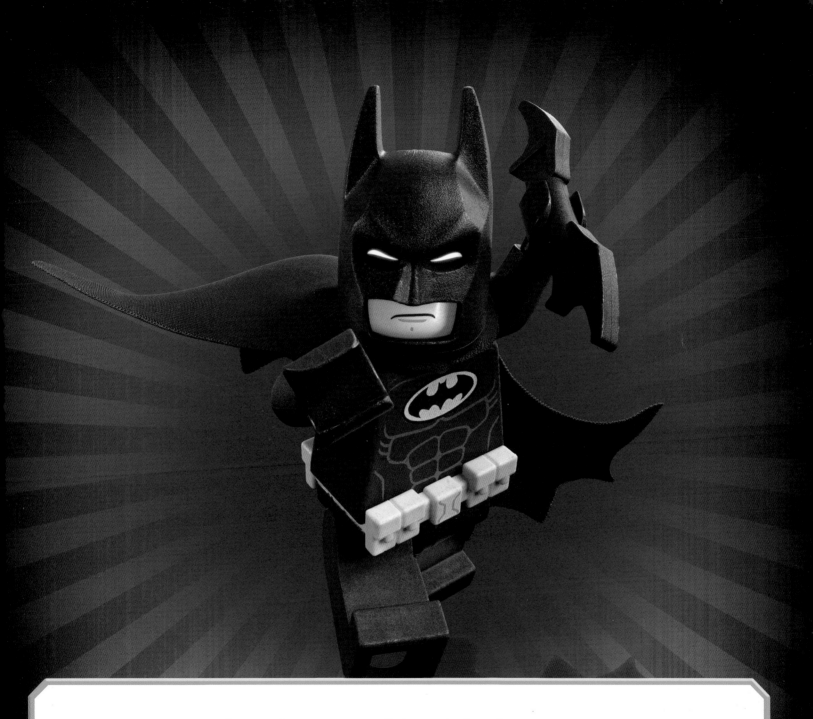

Batman managed to make it to my cell through the chaos.
"I hereby sentence Joker into the Phantom Zone right now!" he shouted.
Just like that, he zapped me with the Phantom Zone Projector and I was gone!

And wouldn't you know it, things just kept getting better!
After Batman broke into Arkham Asylum, the new police commissioner was not too happy with him. She locked him up in my cell! Ha! Ha! Ha!

So here I am, flying into a brand-new world, the Phantom Zone, where I'll learn lots of new tricks! I'm working on a scheme to give Batman the surprise of a lifetime. Ha! Ha! Ha!

Hi. Batman here.

"How did Batman get in this book?" you might ask. "This is the Joker's book!"

Are you serious? I'm here because I'm Batman. There is no way the Joker will ever beat me. I mean, I'm Batman. I'm a night-stalking, crime-fighting vigilante and a heavy-metal rapping machine.

One thing's for certain, the Joker is going down. And he won't know what's hit him. Bring it on!